Folklorist **Hiroshi Naito** was born in Kyoto in 1925. He graduated from Kyoto Junior College of Foreign Languages in 1955 and received a B.A. in Humanities from Ritsumeikan University in 1969. Presently manager of the Kyoto Municipal Education Board's Language Laboratory, he is able to find time outside academic research to pursue his keen interest in things Japanese, especially folklore. Since 1953 he has been writing for the *Mainichi Daily News* about Japanese folklore, history, and literature. The legends in this book were originally published as a series in that newspaper. He is co-author with Harold S. Williams of *The Kamakura Murders of 1864,* which was published recently.

Legends of Japan

Legends of Japan

retold by Hiroshi Naito

illustrations by Masahiko Nishino

CHARLES E. TUTTLE COMPANY

Rutland, Vermont & Tokyo, Japan

Representatives

For Continental Europe:
BOXERBOOKS, INC., Zurich

For the British Isles:
PRENTICE-HALL INTERNATIONAL, INC., London

For Australasia:
PAUL FLESCH & CO., PTY. LTD., Melbourne

For Canada:
M. G. HURTIG, LTD., Edmonton

These legends are printed with permission of the Mainichi
Daily News, *in which they previously appeared.*

Published by the Charles E. Tuttle Company, Inc.
of Rutland, Vermont & Tokyo, Japan
with editorial office at Suido l-chome, 2-6, Bunkyo-ku, Tokyo

Library of Congress Catalog Card No. 73–188013
International Standard Book No. 0-8048-0894-5

First printing, 1972

Table of Contents

• 5 •

Introduction

MOST OF THE stories contained in this book take their material from *Konjaku Monogatari* (Tales, Ancient and Modern) written in the Heian period (794–1185), one of the classical literary masterpieces of Japan, as valued as the works of Shakespeare and Goethe. Unfortunately, however, *Konjaku Monogatari* is less known to foreign readers than the famous *Genji Monogatari* (The Tale of Genji) and *Makura no Soshi* (The Pillow Book), though they were written in the same period. Even among Japanese readers, this work has been hitherto less popular than the latter two, because it was not written in their accomplished style, and in addition it did not deal with such enthralling subjects as gorgeous court life or high society of the day. *Konjaku Monogatari* is composed of thirty-one volumes presenting Japanese, Chinese, and Indian legendary tales, each tale beginning with the familiar phrase "Long, long ago."

The stories range from Buddhist moral tales to humorous anecdotes and fairy tales. A great variety of characters appear in this legendary literature, such as Buddha himself, Shinto deities, noblemen and common people, and even goblins and animals, who act humorously, cruelly, or erotically in the stories. They all live in a world of disorder. The Japanese heroes and heroines live in the chaotic years of the late Heian period, when the nobleman-ruled social structure was being supplanted by the newly budding medieval feudal system. With national police no longer able to exercise authority in the provinces or in the capital, both the nobility and the masses struggled helplessly, their life and property threatened by bands of robbers day and night. In such a state of utter confusion, only the wicked could successfully seize an opportunity to survive, their consciences already paralyzed by evil influences. The honest and weak had no recourse but struggle in the abyss, madly seeking some miserable means of staying alive. Some could protect themselves from danger by using force, by exercising intellect, or by asking the help of merciful Buddha, and some others met a tragic end.

"... for several years, Kyoto had been visited by a series of calamities—earthquake, typhoon, great fire, and famine. And so the capital was deserted. Old records say that shattered wooden images of Buddha or the accessories of household Buddhist shrines, with red lacquer, gold, or silver leaf still sticking to them, were piled up on the roadside and sold for firewood. The whole capital being in such a state, there was, of course, no one who took the least interest in the repair of the decayed Gate of Rashomon. Profiting by the devastation, foxes and other wild animals came to inhabit the gate. Thieves made it their den. Finally it even became customary for people to bring unclaimed corpses to this gate and leave them there. Scared by its ghostliness, the people of Kyoto would not come near the gate after sunset."

Thus a dark picture of the destitute people in the decaying capital was painted by Ryunosuke Akutagawa (1892–1927), a literary genius, in his work *Rashomon,* which took its material from stories contained in *Konjaku Monogatari.* The screenplay for the world-famed Japanese film *Rashomon* was based on a mixture of his two stories, *Rashomon* and *In a Bamboo Grove.*

Konjaku Monogatari was written with an excellent realistic touch and therefore is highly valued as the first example of realism in Japanese prose literature. Though of unknown authorship, it is said to have been written by a court noble named Minamoto Takakuni (1004–1077), or rewritten later using his *Uji Dainagon Monogatari* (The Tales of Uji Dainagon) as the original.

Two of the stories, "The Iron Hat" and "The Lost Dinner," are from a second source, *Tsurezure Gusa* (Jottings of a Hermit), one of the masterworks written in the era of military dictatorhip at Kamakura (1192–1333). It was written by the monk Kenko (1283–1350) around 1330. Popularly called Kenko Hoshi, the monk was of noble birth and versed in Japanese and Chinese classics. He was also a renowned *waka* composer of his time. *Tsurezure Gusa* contains 243 tales, each different in length and indicative of his philosophy. They can be divided into three categories—lessons on life, culture, and miscellaneous observations.

These stories, and illustrations by Masahiko Nishino, were selected from a series originally published in the *Mainichi Daily News*.

—HIROSHI NAITO

1. The
fishermen's battle

LONG, LONG AGO, in the province of Kaga (now Ishikawa Prefecture), there lived a group of seven fishermen who always carried weapons of war, such as bows and arrows, as they went fishing.

One day they went out in a boat, as usual. While they were fishing at sea, black clouds suddenly covered the whole sky and the wind began blowing in violent gusts.

"A storm is coming!"

"Let us return to the shore at once."

They immediately stopped fishing and tried to row their boat with all their strength back to the shore. The wind blew harder and the boat was tossed about by angry waves. All the fishermen felt miserable. They soon found their boat was drifting toward the open sea. Gripping the edge of the boat in order not to be thrown out into the sea, they prayed to Holy Buddha for their safety.

As the storm blew over, the seven men did not know how long they had been adrift. They suddenly sighted an island out on the horizon. "Land!" they cried delightedly, and tried to row their boat toward the island. Strangely, the boat automatically began running toward it as if it were attracted by a magnet. It was not long before their boat reached the island. The fishermen landed on the shore and congratulated one another on their safety.

"What is the name of this island?"

"I have never heard of this island."

"Hey, look! There are many trees heavy with fruit over there."

Though they felt relieved to reach the island, they soon felt uneasy about it. Just then, a good-looking young man suddenly appeared from nowhere and addressed them: "Welcome to you all. I have been expecting your arrival. To tell the truth, it is I who have called you to this island." The fishermen could not understand what the young man had said, so they just stared at one another. One of them said that while fishing, they were overtaken by a storm which blew them to the island. Then the young man said it was he who had caused the storm to blow. At that, the fishermen imagined that he must have been more than an ordinary person, and looked at him nervously.

The young man cried something in the direction from which he had come, and the next instant there appeared many men carrying a chest. As the fishermen opened the chest, they found in it a sumptuous meal which the young man offered to them. Since the fishermen were very hungry, they gratefully ate it all.

Then the young man said, "Now, I want to ask a big favor of you. There is another island far away from here. The king of that island has tried to kill me many times because he wants to take this island from me. Tomorrow he will come again to fight our decisive battle. So, I have called you here to ask for your help."

The fishermen felt very interested in his story and promised that they would be glad to help him win a victory.

"How many men will come with him?"

"Oh, they are not human beings. I am not a human being either. You will find out what I am tomorrow."

The fishermen felt very uneasy about the young man.

He said, "Now, let us work out our fighting plan. When they appear, let them come ashore. Then I will come down from a hill beyond. As I fight the enemy king, I will give you a signal. Then you should immediately shower all your arrows on him. Since my enemy is a strong fighter, please be careful." He added that the battle would start at noon and that they should take their positions on a huge rock near the beach. With that, the young man disappeared into a wood beyond.

The next morning the fishermen took their positions on the rock, as told. In the meantime, black clouds covered the sky, and a strong wind began blowing, and mountainous waves came dashing ashore. They thought the battle would start soon. All of a sudden they saw a couple of big fireballs appear above the horizon, and the next moment these balls began approaching the island. Something was swimming toward them. They soon found it to be a very big centipede about 100 feet long. The fireballs were his sparkling eyes!

Just then, the fishermen heard the grass rustle on the hill beyond, and they saw an enormous serpent come down to the beach.

After glaring at each other for a moment, the animals started a fierce battle, biting each other's bodies. They fought for nearly four hours. As the centipede's feet gave him an advantage, he finally held the serpent down on the ground. The fishermen, who were awaiting the serpent's signal, feared that he would be bitten to death. The serpent soon gave them a "help me" sign, so they showered all the arrows on the victorious centipede, who, though wounded, would not release the serpent. Thereupon the seven fighters assaulted the centipede with their swords, severing all the feet from his body and cutting the body to pieces. Thus the enemy king was killed. Meanwhile, the serpent disappeared from the battleground. The fishermen found their kimonos soaked with the monstrous centipede's blood. After a while, the young man came limping toward them. He looked very tired and on his face were many cuts. He thanked them for their help and burned the centipede's body on the beach.

The young man invited them to live on the fertile island, which produced abundant fruit. It was indeed an attractive invitation, but as the fishermen had left their families in their province, they could not accept it at once. Then the man urged them to bring their families to the island.

"It is really a good invitation. But we don't know how to bring our families here," they said.

"Oh, it is an easy thing to do. I will blow your boat to your country. When you wish to return to this island, you should pray to the Kumata

Shrine for assistance and the deity will blow your boat hither. The shrine is dedicated to my brother," said the serpent-man.

So the fishermen decided to bring their families to the island, and immediately set sail for their country, bidding a temporary farewell to the man. As he had said, their boat was blown by a favorable wind and soon reached the shore of Kaga Province. Their families, which had been worried about them, were very happy to meet them again. The fishermen told them the story, and their families agreed to move to the island. Their neighbors also wished to go with them. One night they sailed from their country in seven boats. As they had prayed to the Kumata Shrine for assistance, the boats were blown by a divine wind and glided over the surface of the sea as swiftly as flying arrows. Soon they reached the island.

Later the settlers named their island "Nekojima" (Cat's Island) and lived their long, happy lives there.

2. Wrestling
a serpent

A LONG TIME ago, in the province of Tango, now the northern part of Kyoto Prefecture, there lived a sumo wrestler of great strength, named Tsuneyo.

Near his house, there was an old marsh. It was not a big marsh, but it was so fathomlessly deep that its bed had never once dried up, even in a long spell of dry weather. Its surface was as smooth as a mirror, and its water very stagnant.

One summer evening, Tsuneyo came out to the edge of this marsh for a stroll. When standing by a big tree, he saw floating weeds before him sway, though there was not even a puff of wind. All of a sudden, the water swelled, and the next moment the head of a huge serpent appeared. An ordinary person would certainly have been paralyzed with terror at such a sight, but Tsuneyo was so stout-hearted that he calmly gazed at it. The serpent also stared at him, shooting out its red tongue and waving it up and down. For a while, they continued this staring match. Then, the serpent turned its head and began to swim across the marsh toward the other side. It was indeed a very horrible sight to see the monstrous serpent swim off, zig-zagging its body, which was as thick as the trunk of a big tree. Since the marsh was not very wide, the tail of the serpent remained on the near side even though its head had reached the other.

Suddenly the creature flung its tail out of the water and extended its end toward the wrestler. The next instant, the monster began to wind its tail around the wrestler's left leg.

"Gosh, this will be fun!" Tsuneyo muttered,

deliberately letting the serpent do what it pleased. The serpent coiled its tail around his leg, from ankle up to knee, and then began to pull him with great force.

"Well, she is going to drag me into the marsh!" he said to himself. He stood firm on the ground by stretching his legs and the serpent continued to pull him. In rivalry with the monster, Tsuneyo stood stauncher than ever before. The serpent with more strength drew the wrestler inch by inch, but the next moment the wrestler pulled back the distance he had lost.

Thus they desperately continued to pull each other for half an hour, when the wrestler's clog straps suddenly snapped. Well, that was the worst possible thing that could have happened!

The wrestler, with his steady posture giving way, was quickly drawn about two or three feet toward the edge of the marsh. But he lost no time taking off the broken clogs to get a steadier footing. His feet gradually rooted into the soil as much as six inches. Another half an hour passed.

When the serpent tried to draw the wrestler with her utmost strength, her tail suddenly snapped off like a straw rope. At that, the wrestler fell on his buttocks with the force of his effort, because he had thrown all the strength of his body into his legs.

"Oh, what a strong monster she is!" he exclaimed. After a while, his pupils came to gather around him. "What's happened, sir?" they asked.

"Nothing. I've just had a contest of strength

with a huge serpent. You should have seen it, boys," Tsuneyo laughingly replied.

"Sir, your left leg . . . " one of them cried, pointing to Tsuneyo's leg. Tsuneyo looked down and found his leg clearly marked with a spiral line. It was the trace of the serpent's coiled tail. There were even some bloodstains on the skin. But the wrestler was as calm as if he knew nothing about what had happened to him.

"The tail of the monster must be around here. You all look for it," he ordered. The pupils searched all over the place and found it in the bushes close by. Its length was well over six feet and its opening was as wide as one foot. It was bluish black and greasy, and presented a forbidding appearance. All the pupils were astonished at the size of the tail.

One day, local citizens who had heard the story asked Tsuneyo how strong the serpent was. Thereupon he had his left leg wound round by a thick rope and let a group of ten men pull it hard. The people asked whether the pullers' strength corresponded to that of the serpent. The wrestler, however, said more men were needed. The people therefore added new hands five by five, and finally the total number of the rope-pullers amounted to sixty. Now the wrestler said flatly that the serpent's strength was as great as that. But, since he had won the contest, his strength was apparently greater than that of the monster. The people thought that Tsuneyo's power must have equalled the strength of at least one hundred men.

3. The lost chance

LONG, LONG AGO, there lived in Kyoto a Buddhist priest who could use magic. For example, he could, with a yell, turn a worn-out straw sandal into a puppy, or he could plunge into the stomach of a horse and come out laughing.

Next door to his temple, there lived a young man who was very envious of the priest's magical power and anxious to learn it. He often asked the priest to teach him this magic, but the priest just smiled off his request. Nevertheless, the young man was too zealous to give up his desire. At last the priest yielded to his entreaties and said, "All right, I will teach you the magic. But in learning it, you have to do several things. First of all, starting today you must purify yourself for a week. Then, make a pail and fill it with red boiled rice. After that, you . . . " the priest, suspiciously looking about, whispered in the young man's ear, "come with me. I will take you to my old teacher of magic."

Now, the young man was very happy. He immediately set to work, purifying himself, making a wooden pail, and filling it with red boiled rice. The day at last came when he was to be taken to the teacher of magic. The priest came by his house, and said, "You must not carry cutlery with you. Its possession is prohibited in learning magic. If you should carry even a small edged tool, your earnest hope would be shattered. Remember that."

"All right. I never will carry any kind of knife as you say," he pledged, "and whatever unreasonable demands the teacher of magic should make of me, I would be happy to meet them if he really teaches me the magic. This is quite a simple request." The young man, however, on reflection felt uneasy that if danger should arise, he would be helpless without a weapon. He therefore had a dagger concealed in his clothes and, pretending it wasn't there, set out together with the priest before day-break.

He followed the priest, carrying the red rice-filled pail on his shoulder, sometimes touching the concealed dagger. The road ran toward a mountain. They went a long way. About noon they reached a fine Buddhist temple at last.

"Wait here," said the priest, and he alone went into the temple. Here in the temple compound, the priest squatted down by the hedge and cleared his throat. Perhaps it was a signal. Presently the door of a temple hall opened from inside and an old priest, popping out his solemn face, asked, "Who is it?"

"It is me, Master," replied the young priest, still keeping himself low.

"Oh, is that you? Come in. I am very pleased to see you again after such a long time. What has brought you here today?"

"Well, Master, it is about my neighbor," replied the young priest, "who is very anxious to learn magic from you."

"Is that so? Where is he?"

Whereupon the younger priest called in the man and presented him to the aged priest. The aspirant humbly offered the pail of red boiled rice to the teacher of magic, who gazed at him.

"Come out, all of you!" the old priest suddenly called in a thunderous voice. "This fellow here appears to have a dagger. Take it from him!"

At that, several acolytes came over to the young man. "Damn bonze! He has seen through me," the man cursed. He thought that should the acolytes examine him they would surely find the dagger; and if so, they would surely beat him to death. He therefore made up his mind to kill the old priest to bear him company to the nether world. Once he determined to do that, he rallied his strength. No sooner had he drawn the dagger and jumped at the priest when the fine temple structure came down with a thunderous roar. And lo! The next moment the aged priest and the fallen structure vanished like smoke. He felt as if he were in a dream.

When he came to his senses, he found himself standing by the young priest in the hall of an old temple. In speechless wonder, he kept standing there for a moment. "Tut!" the priest grumbled, "What a thing you have done!" He disdainfully went on, "You have made the old teacher angry and ruined everything—you have even deprived me of my magical power."

With that, he tramped out. When the young man came out of the temple, he was surprised to find it to be a temple near his house. Why the long journey from dawn to noon? From that time, he never saw the priest again. The young man thus lost forever a chance of learning magic.

4. The reed-mower
and the lady

LONG, LONG AGO, in Kyoto, there lived a poor samurai who had no relatives in the city. Though he served his master well, fortune did not smile upon him. So he often changed his masters, expecting a good position, but he was not rewarded at all for his efforts. In the end he found no person to serve remaining in the city. Thus he was masterless and had to live in dire poverty.

This man had a very beautiful and gentle-hearted wife, who, though poverty stricken, was devoted to her husband. One day he said, "Although I want to live with you forever, our grinding poverty no longer permits our union. So I think it best for us to divorce each other."

The woman was surprised at her husband's sudden proposal and said, "I would like to live with you until death separates us, but this seems impossible now because our union is apparently preventing your advancement. If you really want to divorce me, I shall have to obey you."

Thus they sadly broke up, expecting a happy reunion as soon as possible.

Since the woman had retained her youthfulness and beauty, she was soon employed by a high government official. She was so gentlehearted that she was loved by the family, and after the death of the mistress she was asked by her master to become his wife. Thus the woman married her master and lived a happy life with him in a large mansion. Her new husband was later appointed governor of Settsu Province.

Her former husband became more miserable.

Though he had divorced his wife for advancement, he could not improve his life. Finally he saw that he could no longer obtain any job in the capital and went down to Settsu Province to work as a day laborer. But, as he was well bred, he was not familiar with rough work, so he was sent to mow reeds on the beach.

One day, on the shore of Settsu Sea, a whim of fate brought this man and his divorced wife together. That day the governor of Settsu, accompanied by his family, was on his way to the provincial capital to assume his post. As they came out on the seashore, they were impressed with the scenic beauty and had an outdoor dinner party there.

As the woman was enjoying the party with her family, she by chance saw a decent-looking laborer among many reed-mowers. Though he was poorly dressed, his appearance showed that he must have come of good stock. When she took a good look at him, she found him to be her former husband.

The man was mowing reeds in the water. Finding her former husband working like this, the woman was suddenly touched by his misery and secretly shed tears of sympathy for him. She immediately told a maid to bring the man to her, and when he came she found his kimono quite worn and his arms and legs very dirty with mud. On his legs there were even leeches sucking his blood. She was shocked to see his terrible appearance and told the maid to give him some food, which the man ate greedily before her. Of course, he did not know the kind lady was his divorced wife.

As the man was about to retire from her presence, the woman gave him a kimono with a piece of paper on which she wrote a poem:

> Hoping our happy reunion,
> I parted from you
> in the capital,
> But, why do you mow reeds out here
> on the beach?

The poor man was surprised to read the poem and discover that the kind lady was his divorced wife. He was ashamed of himself and asked for a brush and ink to compose a poem in reply:

> Since our separation,
> I have been more badly off.
> And, recalling our old days,
> I find my present position more
> intolerable.

Reading his reply, the lady became more sympathetic, but she knew her present position did not permit her to help him in any way. The man, deeply ashamed of his misery, went away, no longer returning to his work.

This story was told by the lady in her later years.

5. The iron hat

THIS IS AN old story of the priests of Ninna-ji Temple in Kyoto. Once, when an altar boy became a priest the whole membership of the temple had a feast to celebrate his taking orders. They all drank and made merry. While they were thus holding high jinks, the new priest took up a three-legged iron pot close by and playfully put it on his head. As the pot fitted him tightly, he, flattening his nose, pulled it even below his chin and began to dance. His blind dancing was so waggish that they all burst out laughing. When the merriment was over after a while, the new priest tried to pull off the pot, but in vain! It caught his ears and nose and would not come off.

"Hey, take it off!" he cried.

His voice was muffled and resounded in the pot so that the other priests could not hear exactly what he said.

They became anxious and pulled the pot by the legs as hard as they could. But the pot still would not come off. The priest's neck, having been rubbed by the edge of the pot, became bruised.

"Oh! I am choked. Take it off. Quick!" he cried again.

"Say, I have a good idea. Let's break the pot," said one of the group. With that, they struck the pot hard with a hammer, but the pot-bearer could not stand their shower of blows.

Whereupon they took him to a physician in town. The doctor was surprised to see such a strange patient. He said he was very sorry he did not know how to treat the patient, because he had no experience in handling such an unusual case. The priests were helpless so they took the pot-headed priest back to the temple and let him lie in bed.

His old mother, friends, and relatives were immediately sent for. They came and gathered at his bedside. His mother wept and grieved but the pot-wearing priest could not hear her tearful voice.

At last some one suggested, "Let's pull it off by force, even though his ears and nose might be torn off. That is the only way left for us. I don't think it will cost his life."

After that, they put in straw around his head so the pot might come off easily. Grabbing its legs, they pulled the pot so hard it seemed his head might be torn off at any moment. After some struggle, the pot finally came off, but the priest's nose and ears were injured.

We are told that, although he was cured of this peculiar sickness, he afterward suffered from these injuries and had to lie in bed for a long time.

6. The demon's spittle

A LONG TIME ago there was in Kyoto a young, very pious man. He often visited Rokkaku-do (Hexagonal Shrine) to offer his devout prayer to Kannon-sama (Goddess of Mercy) enshrined there.

Once he called on a friend on New Year's Eve. When he left this friend's house, it was already dark. On his way home, as he was crossing Modoribashi (Returning Bridge), he saw many people approaching, carrying blazing torches. He thought it was a lord and his attendants, so he got out of their way by hiding himself under the bridge. Soon they were on the bridge. The man wondered who the lord could be. He put his head out from under the bridge and looked up. And lo! They were not human beings. They were all *oni* (demons) with a pair of horns on each head. Some of them were single-eyed, while others had several hands each, and still others were one-legged. He was horrified at this sight.

"Hey, there's a human being down there," one of the *oni* suddenly cried. "Let's catch him," said another. In a moment, the man was a prisoner. He feared they would eat him and resigned himself to their next action. But there was no indication of any cruelty. Presently one of them said the man was not fit to eat and thrust him away. Then they spat in his face and went off. The man now felt relieved to have his life spared. He went home in a hurry. When he reached his house, his family would not speak to him, although they looked directly at him.

"Why do you keep such silence?" he asked. But they ignored him. The man wondered what was the matter with them. After a while, there suddenly flashed into his mind the idea that the *oni*'s spittle must have made his figure invisible. He could see his family and hear what they said, but they seemed to be unable to see or hear him. Now he was at a loss.

The next day was New Year's Day. His family, however, were unhappy because of the missing man. He fretfully shouted to them that he was with them in the house, but in vain. Although he patted his children on their heads, they did not seem to feel his hand. As the day passed, they began to sob for their father, thinking that he must have been spirited away. New Year's Day thus became a tragic day for them. Several days passed. The man thought that for him there was no other way left but to ask the merciful goddess for her help. Thereupon he immediately visited Rokkaku-do Shrine.

"Oh, merciful Kannon-sama, please make my body visible to my family. Please have mercy on me!" He offered fervent prayers to the goddess for two full weeks.

On the last night in retreat, as he was praying, he unintentionally fell asleep and had a dream. In the vision he met a holy Buddhist priest who came from behind a bamboo curtain and solemnly said, "Ho there, my faithful follower! You leave here tomorrow morning and do what you're told by the first person you meet on your way home.

Follow my directions and you will be restored!"
At that he prostrated himself before the priest.
When he awoke from his sleep, it was already
light.

He left the shrine and did not go far before he
met a cattleman. He thought this was the person
referred to by Kannon-sama. The cattleman
approached him and said, "Hello, my dear friend,
come with me." The unhappy man was pleased
to think that he must have been made visible to
others, and therefore he immediately followed the
cattleman. They went a little way and arrived at
the front gate of a big mansion. The cattleman
tied his ox to a tree close by and opened the gate
slightly and motioned to the man to follow him
in. The invisible man said it was impossible to do
that, because the chink was too narrow for him to
pass through. Upon that, the cattleman angrily
dragged him in by the hand. How strange! He
could pass through the chink as freely as the wind.
He felt as if he were still in a dream.

The cattleman led farther into the courtyard.
At last they came into a rear chamber where a
beautiful princess of the mansion was sick in bed
attended by her parents—a lord and a lady—and
many maids who were all concerned about her
illness. They did not even notice the entry of these
invisible intruders—you must realize now that the
cattleman was also invisible to ordinary persons.
The unhappy man realized his figure was still
invisible and became more discouraged. The
cattleman told him to hit the sick princess on the

head with a wooden hammer. The man did as he was told. Every time he struck at her, she writhed in agony. At that, the lord and the lady believed that their daughter would soon die. They immediately sent for a Buddhist priest to expel evil spirits from the sick.

Shortly after, a fine priest came and practiced exorcism. He chanted a Buddhist prayer which prevented the faithful intruder from continuing his violence. The priest then chanted another prayer. At that, the pious invisible intruder's kimono suddenly caught fire, and it blazed up. Now, he was astonished. "Fire, Fire!" he cried, madly rolling about on the floor. The next moment his figure suddenly became visible. Those in the room were astonished and all asked, "Where did he come from?"

The guards came in and caught the man. The lord in person questioned him about his abrupt appearance there. The man told the lord of his strange adventure. Whereupon the priest said, "That is a miracle. Perhaps Kannon-sama of Rokkaku-do Shrine has meant to reveal this person's figure and also cure the princess." It was indeed miraculous that when the man's figure was disclosed, the princess recovered at the same time.

The man went home happily. Needless to say, all his family were delighted to see him again.

The identity of the cattleman must remain a mystery, but many people believe he was another spirit.

7. A piece of straw

LONG, LONG AGO, there lived in Kyoto a young man who had no kith or kin in the town. One day he visited Hase Temple in Yamato Province to pray to Kannon (Goddess of Mercy).

"O merciful Kannon-sama! Please give me your mercy. Since I am in dire poverty, I have nothing to eat. I shall starve to death soon. If I must starve, I would like to do it here in your presence. Please take pity on me and tell me how to live." So praying, the young man prostrated himself before the image of Kannon.

The temple priests, who saw him daily praying for something, talked about him:

"Look! That poor man is praying again today."

"I wonder what he is praying for so earnestly."

"He looks very pale. Maybe he is hungry."

"If he should starve to death there, we shall have trouble in clearing off his body."

One of them approached the poor man and asked what he was praying for. Then the man replied that he wanted the mercy of Kannon-sama, and that he would not move an inch until the goddess gave it to him.

The priests admired him for his enthusiastic praying and gave him meals so that he might not die of hunger. Thus the young man continued praying day after day.

On the night of the twenty-first day, when his term of worship was to expire, the man dozed off. In his dream a noble-looking Buddhist priest appeared and addressed him: "You are suffering now because you committed many sins before you came into this world. So you will not be given the mercy of Kannon. But you are so earnestly praying for her mercy that I will give you a small gift. When you leave this temple you will pick up something. That is what I give you. So you must not throw it away. Follow my directions and you will be all right."

With that, the priest disappeared and the man came to himself. He thought that the priest must have been Kannon-sama in disguise. So he at once left the temple for home, bidding farewell to the kind temple priests who gave him a package of rice balls for lunch.

As he came a little way from the temple he suddenly stumbled over a stone. When he tried to raise himself he found something in his right hand. "What is it?" he wondered.

It was a piece of straw.

"A piece of straw! Let me see. . . . Oh, yes, this must be what Kannon-sama has bestowed upon me." So, instead of throwing it away, he carefully put it into his pocket and went on farther.

As he was passing by a paddy field a bee came flying from somewhere and buzzed about his head. Though he beat at it again and again, it still came back to him, so he angrily caught it and tied it with the straw to the end of a twig he had in hand. But the bee went on buzzing with the straw attached to it.

It was not long before he met an ox-drawn court carriage attended by a group of men. Riding in the vehicle were a court lady and her little son.

Seeing the bee, the boy wanted it so earnestly that the lady politely asked the traveler to give her son the insect.

The poor man, though unwillingly, gave the bee to the boy, who then became very happy with the insect. In return for the bee, the lady gave him three oranges wrapped in a sheet of paper. The man was very happy to find that the piece of straw had now turned into three oranges and he hung them from the twig.

The sun was shining very brightly. Soon the young man came across a group of travelers—a beautiful lady and her servants. She appeared quite exhausted from walking under the burning sun. As a matter of fact, she was very thirsty and badly wanted a drink of water. But since they found neither a well nor a pond around, the servants did not know where to find any.

One of them asked the young man where they could get drinking water for their mistress. Then the man, replying that no water could be obtained around there, asked why they needed it. They told him that they were on their way to Kannon Temple with their mistress, who was very thirsty.

Hearing that, the man felt very sorry for her and offered them his oranges to appease her thirst. They gratefully received them and took them to the lady who was resting by the road. She was so thirsty that she ate them all in a moment and expressed her deep gratitude to the poor man. In return for his kindness, she gave him silks.

The man was very happy to receive the fine goods and expressed his thanks to the merciful goddess, who had now turned the gift of straw into silks. That night he sought a night's lodging in a farmhouse.

Early next morning he left the house to continue his journey and before he went a long way he ran across a samurai on horseback accompanied by a group of footmen. Since it was a fine horse, the young man stood still to watch it. All of a sudden the animal fell down and died for no apparent reason. The samurai, who was very surprised at the sudden death of his favorite horse, mounted a second to continue his trip. And he told his retainers to clear away the body of his dead animal.

The man, witnessing this scene, promptly proposed to exchange the dead horse for his silk goods. Since the footmen were at a loss as to the means of clearing away the animal, they accepted his offer and went away with the silks.

Left alone, he said to himself:

"A piece of straw, which I had received from Kannon-sama, turned into three oranges at first, then into silk goods, and now into a dead horse. I am sure Kannon-sama will soon bring this dead animal back to life."

He purified himself by washing his hands and rinsing his mouth and prayed to the goddess: "O merciful Kannon-sama! Please bring this dead horse back to life at once. It must be what you have bestowed upon me."

Behold!

The dead animal suddenly opened its closed eyes and raised its head. At this sight the poor man was greatly delighted and helped the animal rise to its feet. Thanking Kannon-sama for her mercy, he immediately took the horse into a wood by the road to give it a good rest. The animal soon regained strength, and so the man continued his journey to Kyoto riding on the horse.

When he came into a village near Kyoto, he saw a wealthy family busily preparing themselves for a journey. The man thought: "If I should be seen riding on such a fine horse in the capital, I should be mistaken for a horse thief and arrested by the police. It seems better to sell this horse to that family who will perhaps need it for their trip."

Whereupon he immediately got off his horse and asked the family if they would buy it. Admiring the animal, the master of the family said that he had never seen such a fine horse and proposed to buy it at once. But as payment for the horse, he gave the man his vast paddy fields. Therefore the young man had to settle down in the village. From that day on he worked very hard on the farm, which produced plenty of rice crops in autumn. Many years later he at last became the richest farmer in the village. Thanking Kannon-sama for her tender mercy, he lived a happy life with his family.

8. The hunter's trick

LONG, LONG AGO, in the province of Mimasaka (Okayama Prefecture), there was a small Shinto shrine called Takano Jinja. It was dedicated to Monkey and Serpent. Every year the shrine celebrated a festival, and it was the customary practice to offer a human sacrifice to the deities on the occasion of the festival. This custom had been practiced continuously from time immemorial. The sacrifice was a pretty girl chosen from among the daughters of the people living in the province. Therefore, as the festival came near, the parents of all daughters became restless, wondering who should be the victim of the year.

One year, a sixteen-year-old girl was chosen as a sacrifice. She was the only daughter of an old couple, who loved her so dearly that they wept bitterly over their hapless fate. From the day of selection the daughter and her parents bewailed their ill fortune day and night, numbering the decreasing days of their union at home. It was the practice that the chosen girl be fed attentively until the time of feasting.

One day an "Inuyama" hunter visited this province. The Inuyama was a brave hunter who used a pack of hounds in hunting wild boars and deer in the mountains.

This hunter became very sympathetic with the sorrowful family and offered them his help. He said he would be glad to take her place in the festival, and told them to hang sacred festoons about the house and to keep themselves away from the villagers. Then he selected two strong hounds from among his dogs and trained them to fight monkeys. He also sharpened his sword for a fight.

The day of feasting came around at last, and the shrine priests and the villagers came to take the girl to the shrine. They had a big wooden chest to contain the sacrifice. Taking the place of the girl, however, the hunter, who was wearing her kimono and carrying a sword, secretly hid himself in the chest. He also had the two hounds hidden in it. The girl's parents, as planned, pretended to wail over their sad farewell to the departing chest, so no one imagined that the box contained the hunter and his dogs. The villagers unwittingly carried the chest to the shrine at the foot of a sacred mountain.

Meanwhile, the old couple and their daughter at home were uneasy, thinking that should the deities find the sacrifice to be the wrong person, they would punish the whole family.

The villagers carrying the chest soon reached the shrine, where they solemnly held a rite to offer the sacrifice to the deities. Then they opened the old door of the shrine, put in the chest, and closed the door. And in front of the shrine they waited attentively to see what would happen to the chest.

When left behind in the shrine, the hunter opened the cover of the chest slightly and looked out. And lo! Right in front of an altar was seated a big monkey about seven feet tall. The animal looked very happy with the human sacrifice. On each side of him were about fifty small monkeys, who cried something in their language. A big chopping board and a big knife were placed before the boss monkey, who would cut the sacrifice and eat it.

When the boss monkey stood up laboriously and tried to open the chest, the hunter sent out the hounds to battle with the monkeys and he himself jumped out with his sword. The hounds attacked the big monkey furiously and bit him. The boss monkey received many wounds and fell down there. Then the hunter dragged him up to the chopping board and said: "As you ate many girls, I will kill you as punishment and let my dogs eat you up. Now, prepare for death!"

The boss monkey cried for help, with his hands clasped before his eyes, and apologized, "Please forgive me for what I have done. I promise you I will never eat people again. So please spare my life!"

"Shut up!" the hunter cried, and tried to kill him. Meanwhile the two hounds killed some small monkeys and other monkeys ran away for their lives.

While the priests and villagers were anxiously waiting, the chief priest suddenly started running about wildly as if he had gone mad. Then he said solemnly, "Listen, you all! I am deity of the shrine. I do not want sacrifices any more. Today I have decided to stop eating girls. Now I have been caught by a hunter who will kill me. So, help me." So saying, the priest fainted away.

"The deity must have entered into the priest!"

the villagers cried, and ran into the shrine, where they found the hunter ready to kill the big monkey. They told him of the divine message and asked him to forgive the animal, but the hunter would not meet their request, saying that the monkey must pay dearly for what he had done.

"Through the mouth of the priest, I have said I would never eat people again. So, please do not kill me," the big monkey entreated. Whereupon the hunter reluctantly freed the monkey, which ran away into the mountain.

It is said that the hunter later married the sacrificial girl and lived a happy life with her.

9. No melon to spare

LONG, LONG AGO, one summer day, a caravan of horses was traveling along the highway between Yamato Province and Kyoto, capital of this country. Each horse carried many watermelons. From olden times Yamato Province was noted for its watermelons. The caravan was on its way to a market in Kyoto.

It was very hot. As the caravan came near the capital, one of the horse drivers proposed a rest on the roadside. And they halted their horses in the shade of a big tree and put down the burdens from the sweating backs of the animals.

"I am thirsty. Let's eat a watermelon," one of them said. The others were also thirsty, so they agreed to his suggestion. They immediately sliced a watermelon and ate it.

As they were thus quenching their thirst, an old man appeared. He wore a summer kimono and straw sandals, and was carrying a cane. He silently stood by the drivers and watched them eat the watermelon. He looked quite tired and after a while, he humbly asked for some.

"We're very sorry for you, old man. Though we carry so many watermelons here, we have none to spare," one of the drivers said.

Then, the old man said, "It's very unkind of you to keep an old man thirsty under the burning sun. If you cannot spare me even a slice, I will grow many watermelons here and eat them."

"Grow many watermelons here!" the drivers laughed.

The old man set to work at once. He picked up

a piece of wood and dug up the ground with it as if to plow the fields.

"What's he going to do?"

"He's turning up the soil as if to plant seeds."

"He must have gone mad."

The old man soon finished his digging work. Then he picked up the seeds of the watermelon which the drivers scattered all over the place, and sowed them in the soil. After a second or two, small leaves turned out of the planted seeds.

"How strange!" the drivers exclaimed.

The small leaves began to grow and soon they became dense. Before the drivers winked their eyes, they sent out buds and turned into the shapes of watermelons which soon began to grow bigger and at last became fine watermelons. The ill-natured drivers, who saw this strange show, were impressed with the old man's magic.

"He might be a kami-sama [a deity]," they thought. And they were struck with awe.

The old man took up one of the fresh watermelons and ate it with gusto. He proudly said, "As you did not spare me a single slice, I have grown them. As I cannot eat them all, you eat too." So saying, the old man picked up some of them and gave them to the amazed drivers. There were so many watermelons there that they could not eat all of them. So the old man invited passersby to eat them. Since it was very hot, all the persons were delighted with the nice present and gratefully ate watermelons on the road. Before long, they had eaten them all.

"Well, it's time to go," the old man said, and went on his way.

"Let's start, too," the drivers said, and prepared to resume their trip.

"No watermelons!" one of them suddenly cried. The others were also stunned to find their watermelons gone from the baskets.

"They're all gone!"

"How strange!"

"Could such a thing be possible?"

They intently looked for their missing watermelons all over the place, but in vain. The watermelons had all disappeared. The drivers, holding their arms, wondered where their watermelons had gone.

"I suppose the old man took them out of the baskets. Perhaps he played a trick on us in order to keep our eyes off the watermelons."

"I never thought our own watermelons were being eaten up. He must be a magician, indeed."

"Yes, quite a magician! I wonder where he's gone. Well, without the watermelons it's not necessary to go to the market, so let's go back to Yamato."

Thus they agreed to return home. They turned around their horses and went their way back to the province of Yamato.

"They grudged giving only a slice and lost all," a bystander laughed. All the persons who had witnessed this interesting event were mystified by the old man's magic.

10. A water sprite

LONG, LONG AGO, in the capital, an ex-emperor lived in a very large palace named Reizei-in. After the emperor's death, the Reizei-in palace was opened to the public. One-half of its premises was turned into a residential section, and in the other half there was a big pond. Before long many houses mushroomed around this pond.

One summer evening, when it was very sultry, people living in these houses came out on the verandas facing the pond to enjoy the cool air. All of a sudden an old man about three feet tall appeared from nowhere and passed his hand over their faces. They felt a chill creep over them, but they pretended to be unaware of his presence. The queer old man did nothing else and just went away.

"Who is he? What on earth is he?" they asked after seeing the old man. He stood on the edge of the pond, and the next moment his figure suddenly vanished into thin air.

"Wherever did he go? Beyond the edge there is nothing but water!" they wondered. The pond was so old, with various weeds in it, that it appeared very forbidding.

"He must be the spirit of the pond!" they imagined. From that night on, the strange old man came out nightly to feel their faces. This strange story soon spread all over the capital.

"Every night a mysterious old man appears to feel the faces of the people who are enjoying the cool air by the pond."

"Really? What is he?" they asked.

One day a brave young samurai declared he would catch the old man, and as the evening came he took his position by the pond pretending to be enjoying the cool air. He had a rope to tie the old man with. In the early evening the old man did not make his appearance.

"Tut!" the samurai grumbled. "He is not likely to come out this evening." Bored with doing nothing, he soon dozed off. Shortly after midnight, however, he suddenly felt someone passing a hand over his face and so he quickly pounced upon the rogue and tied him up. Then he cried, "Hey! Come out, all of you. I've caught him!" A crowd of people soon gathered about the mysterious creature. Under the light of a torchfire they found a poor old man about three feet tall, dressed in a worn-out, yellow kimono. He blinked his eyes, for he seemed surprised.

"Who are you?"

"Where did you come from?" they attacked him with many questions all at once, but the old man just remained silent. After a short while, however, he smiled and said in a low voice, "Will you please bring me a basin full of water?"

Whereupon they brought a big basin full of water and put it before the strange old man. Then, letting his face reflect on the surface of the water, the man declared solemnly,

"Now, listen. I am the Water Sprite!"

With that, he jumped into the water and his figure soon faded away into it. Next moment the water suddenly swelled up in the basin. It was strange, indeed! In the water nothing remained but the rope, with which the old man had been tied.

At this sight the people knew that the stranger was really the Water Sprite. They carefully carried the water-filled basin to the edge of the pond and poured the water into it.

From that night on, it was said that the old man never made his appearance again around the pond.

11. The ogre's horses

LONG, LONG AGO, a company of three Buddhist priests were going about the country for the practice of Buddhistic austerities. They wore black robes and big straw hats and carried canes and small bells. Ringing the bells, they visited from door to door to offer prayers. In return for this service, they received alms. When night fell, they slept in the open air or asked for a night's lodging.

After they made the rounds of the mainland, they went across the sea to Shikoku Island and visited villages on the seashore.

One day they took the wrong way and found themselves in mountains. They thought that as they had been traveling along the coastline to their right, they would come out on the seashore if they continued. So they went to the right, but they only went deeper into the mountains. The sun had already set and it was dark all around. And they became very hungry.

The priests still kept walking because they thought they would be eaten up by wolves if they should sleep under the stars. As they went farther they saw a light in the distance and went straight to it. After some time they found themselves in front of an old house. They immediately asked for admission, but no answer came. Silence prevailed all about the place, and the priests felt uneasy, imagining that the house might be inhabited by man-eating monsters. But they were so tired that they had no choice but to ask for lodging there that night.

Knocking on the door, they asked for admission

again. This time a big voice answered and an old priest about sixty years old stuck out his head. They were stunned to see this priest, who had black sparkling eyes, a big mouth and hands, and looked grim enough to eat them up in a moment.

"Do come in and rest yourselves," said the old priest kindly.

The three priests were shown into the drawing room, where a fire was burning in the hearth. The old priest prepared a meal for them, and since they were so hungry they ate it all greedily. After they finished the meal, the host called in his servant, who looked even grimmer than the master.

"We have three guests tonight, so bring 'them' here," said the old priest. Then the servant grinned and retired to the next room.

"What are 'them'?" asked one priest.

"What is he going to do with 'them'?" asked another.

The three priests waited restlessly to see what was going to take place in the room. The servant soon came back with a whip and horse bridles. They wondered what he would use them for.

"Let us begin at once," the old priest said.

"Which one shall we start with, Master?" asked the servant.

"Any one you like," the master replied.

Then the servant picked up one of the three visitors and threw him out into the garden. The other two priests were amazed at his giant strength and fearfully watched what he was going to do

with their fellow priest. The servant immediately
started whipping him. "Oh! Help me!" the victim
cried. The priest was whipped as many as fifty
times and his screams finally became almost in-
audible. The monstrous servant then took off the
priest's kimono and whipped his naked body
another fifty times, and he fainted.

"That's enough. Pick him up!" the master
said. When the servant tried to pull up the fainted
one, the priest suddenly rose to his feet neighing.
And lo! He was now turned into a fine horse and
shook his head several times, pawing the ground
with his hoof. The other priests were astonished
to see him. Then the servant put the bridle on
him and led him away to the stable.

"The host is a monster. We shall soon be turned
into horses. What shall we do?" the two priests
thought.

The servant soon came back and resumed his
peculiar work on the second priest, who was also
turned into a horse and led away to the stable.
Now, the third priest earnestly prayed to Buddha
for help.

When the servant came back again from the
stable, the master told him to stop for a while and
they retired to the next room for a rest. They bade
the third one to stay where he was. The survivor
now had to find some way to escape from the
devil's house. The next moment, however, a big
voice came saying, "You are staying where you
are?" The priest immediately answered the voice.
Again the voice said, "Go and see if the paddy

fields behind the house are filled with water."

The priest could not understand why the voice had asked such a queer question, but he immediately examined the fields. After some time he heard snores which were as loud as thunder.

"Now is the time to escape. Oh, Hotoke-sama, please protect me from the monsters," he prayed. He stole cautiously out of the house and ran as fast as he could. After running for some time he saw a lighted house in the distance and went straight toward it.

When he came near the house he found someone standing in front of it. He instinctively thought that the house might also be a monster's den. But as he tried to run away, someone suddenly called him. It was a woman.

"Who are you?"

"I am an itinerant priest. I have just come from an ogre's house where my friends were turned into horses," the priest said.

The woman kindly showed him into her house and asked if the ogre had told him to examine the paddy fields. The priest was surprised at her question and replied yes. Then she told him that the ogre had intended to bury him alive in the fields. She added that the ogre was none other than her father, and she promised that she would be glad to help him escape from the danger. Then the woman advised him to seek shelter at her sister's and wrote a letter of introduction to her.

With that, the priest visited her sister. But, before long, there was someone knocking on the door, and the woman told him to hide quickly in a closet. Then he heard a big voice telling her to open the door. The priest in the closet trembled with fear, for the door was soon opened and some-one came into the house.

"Did the bonze come here?"

It was the ogre's voice. He talked with the woman for some time and then went away. She opened the closet and told the priest to run as far away as possible.

"You are the only person to escape from the ogre. You are very lucky," the woman said.

The priest, who deeply appreciated her kindness, immediately left for the human world.

12. The dragon king's palace

LONG, LONG AGO, in the capital, there lived a yo
samurai, whose name still remains unknown—
probably because he was an insignificant samurai.
This samurai was a pious man. On the eighteenth
day of each month, which was the day of worship-
ing Kannon, he abstained from animal food and
visited the Buddhist temples in the capital.

One day when he was on his way to a temple
on the eastern outskirts of the capital, he came
across an old man carrying a cane. He saw a little
snake hanging from the end of this man's cane,
and the snake was moving its body.

"Where are you going, old man?" asked the
young samurai.

"To the capital, sir," replied the old man.

"Why are you carrying the snake?"

"I have a particular reason."

"Couldn't you set it free? Today is Kannon's
day, so it is a sin to kill an animal on such a day."

"Though I don't want to kill the snake, I have
to do it to earn my living. I think Kannon-sama
will forgive my sin."

"What do you use the snake for?" asked the
samurai.

"I need the snake's grease in making maces.
I make my living by selling maces."

"Oh, I see. Then how about exchanging your
snake for my outer kimono?"

The old man gladly accepted the samurai's
offer and they immediately exchanged their goods.

As the young man was about to go, the old
man told him that he had caught the snake in

a pond a little way off. So the samurai at once went to the pond and released the snake in the water. Then he resumed his pilgrimage to the Buddhist temple. As he went some distance from the pond, he met a pretty girl about twelve years old.

"Why is a girl at such a lonely place?" he wondered.

"Hello!" she said. "I was waiting for you here."

"For what?"

"To say thank you. Because you saved my life. My parents also want to express their gratitude to you, so I am here to take you to them."

The samurai now realized that the girl was the little snake he had saved. The girl at once led him back to the pond, where she asked him to wait for her for a time. And behold! Suddenly she vanished into the pond.

But soon she reappeared and told him to close his eyes for a moment. When he opened his eyes again, he found himself standing in front of the big gate of a magnificent castle. The girl immediately showed him into the castle, and he was surprised to see all rooms and halls studded with jewels. It was like a fairyland.

Soon an old man of dignity, about seventy years of age, with a long white beard, appeared before him and showed him into the most gorgeous chamber, where he thanked the young man for his kindness in saving his daughter's life. He said that although he had always told her not to play in the pond, she would not heed his warning and at last was caught.

The old man and his family entertained him handsomely with all kinds of delicacies. He said, "I am the Dragon King. I wish to present you with a treasure in return for your kindness." So saying, he took a piece of golden rice cake out of the treasure box. He divided it in two and gave one piece to the samurai. He said, "Whenever you need money, you break it and use a part of it. You will never be out of money."

The samurai accepted his gift thankfully and bade farewell to the Dragon King. The girl accompanied him to the front gate and told him to close his eyes again. When he opened them, he found himself standing by the pond. She again thanked him and disappeared into the water.

Back in the capital, he used the golden rice cake, which, though he broke it, soon attained its original size. Before long, he became a rich man.

After his death, however, this treasure mysteriously vanished, so it was not handed down to posterity.

13. The bishop's kick

LONG, LONG AGO, there lived in Kyoto an old bishop named Kancho. He was the chief priest of Ninna-ji Temple. A man of noble origin, he was highly learned, virtuous, and also quite vigorous.

Once Kancho had some parts of the temple structure repaired. Many men worked very hard every day on scaffoldings and ladders. Kancho sometimes went his rounds to inspect the work. One evening, after all the workers had gone home, he came out alone to the site. He walked around the place for a while, and when he was going back to his quarters, there suddenly stood in his way a man dressed in black with a black hood. As it was already dark, Kancho could not tell who this man was.

"Who is this?" Kancho asked calmly. The strange man replied threateningly:

"Heh! heh! As you see, I am a pauper. I want your fine kimono, and so I am here before your very eyes."

He seemed to have a drawn sword behind his back. Kancho, however, was not surprised at all. Still very calm, he said, "So you are a pauper? Poor fellow! But don't you know how to beg for mercy? Such impoliteness! I shall have to mend your ways." No sooner had he uttered the words than he kicked the man with crushing force.

The man had no time to express his surprise at Kancho's quick action and the next moment he disappeared up into the air. Kancho, wondering where the man had gone, went back to his quarters, called together his acolytes, and told them the story. At that, the acolytes got excited and ran out to catch the shameless fellow, each armed with a club and a lantern. They searched for the robber all over the place, but in vain.

"There he is!" one of them cried suddenly, pointing his finger upward. They all looked up, and lo! High up, on the top of the scaffoldings, was hanging something that looked like a human being. They all immediately ran up to the spot, and found the robber dangling from a bar there. He was insensible and had bruises on his body.

The acolytes took him off the bar and angrily dragged him down to the ground. When hauled before the bishop, the robber was very humble.

"You, black gentleman," addressed Kancho tenderly, "remember forever that your unwise attempt to assault me has made you smart for it! Be a good man from now on."

With that, Kancho quickly took off his warm kimono and gave it to the robber. The acolytes watched amazed at all that their master did. The robber, gratefully received the kimono and disappeared into the darkness.

This story of Kancho's mercy was handed down to posterity at Ninna-ji Temple. Those who later heard it were surprised at the bishop's great strength in having kicked a robber high up into the sky. They were sure that the robber, in falling, must have been caught by a bar of the scaffolding. It is said that the many vigorous priests of this temple in later days must surely be successors of Kancho.

14. The
long-nosed goblins

LONG, LONG AGO, there was in China a bumptious *tengu* named Chira Eiju. A *tengu* is a red, long-nosed goblin who is possessed of magic powers. Although it looks like a human being, it has a pair of big wings on its back and can fly as freely as a bird. Japanese *tengu* were represented by Sojo-bo of Mt. Kurama, Taro-bo of Mt. Atago, and Jiro-bo of Mt. Hiei—all these mountains rising around Kyoto.

Once Chira Eiju, flying over the seas and mountains, came to Japan to call on Jiro-bo of Mt. Hiei. When talking with Jiro-bo, Chira Eiju boasted, "In my country, there is no one who can beat my magic power. Even a great magician priest is no match for me." The Japanese call a braggart a *tengu*. Chira Eiju could indeed be called a perfect *tengu*. He triumphantly boasted of his supernatural power, wriggling his long nose.

"Although I have often heard about you, I did not know that you are such a great *tengu*," said Jiro-bo admiringly.

At that, Chira Eiju, feeling more proud, went on, "Such being what I am, Japanese magician priests are all beneath my notice. Well, my dear Jiro-bo, shall I show you the great power of my magic?"

"Oh, yes, please."

"All right. Come with me!"

They immediately went out to the busiest path on the mountain. There, Chira Eiju meant to throw a spell over passers-by. Jiro-bo, being a well-known person in the mountains, hid himself behind a big tree and watched what the Chinese *tengu* was going to do.

"Are you ready, dear Jiro-bo? Now watch me!" So saying, he quickly turned into the figure of an old Buddhist priest. In that shape, he meant to await the arrival of his victim. After a while, along came a high priest named Yokei.

"Here he comes!" Jiro-bo cried at the sight of the priest, and intently watched what Chira Eiju would do with him. He imagined the Chinese *tengu* would have the priest walk on his hands, or turn him into a frog or a worm. Second after second, time elapsed; but nothing happened to the priest. Priest Yokei just walked briskly away, looking as if nothing was the matter with him.

Jiro-bo was not a little disappointed. "I say, dear Chira Eiju, what's wrong?" he asked, turning his head toward the Chinese goblin, and was surprised to see . . . no Chira Eiju there! "Hey, where are you?" When Jiro-bo looked in the distance by shading his eyes with his hand, he found the Chinese *tengu* hanging upside down from a tall tree in the valley.

"My dear Chira Eiju, what are you doing down there?" yelled Jiro-bo.

"O dear, dear! Whoever is that monk?"

"He is a famous mountaineering ascetic named Yokei. Perhaps he is on his way to the Imperial Palace to offer a prayer," Jiro-bo replied. "I expected you would have that famous priest spin himself round and round like a top."

Chira Eiju mumbled with a shudder, "Gosh!

He beat me. When I saw him coming along, I rejoiced thinking 'Here comes my fellow!' But in a moment, his figure turned into a great flame and it came near me. I was almost burnt. He threw a spell of fire over me."

"Well, don't be discouraged. Try again," Jiro-bo urged.

Chira Eiju again turned himself into the figure of an old priest. Presently there came a high priest named Jinzen, riding on a palanquin, attended by a page with a cane in his hand.

"Here he comes!"

Chira Eiju had scarcely rejoiced at the arrival of his second prey, when the page turned to him and sharply shouted at him, "You rude fellow!"

That was enough. Boastful Chira Eiju once again was blown off to a distance.

"You were beaten again, dear Chira Eiju."

"Yes, but what's the matter with me today," wondered the Chinese goblin, obstinately refusing to acknowledge his defeat.

"Whoever was he? Pretending to be asleep on the palanquin, that bonze was secretly offering an exorcizing prayer. He even had a strong bodyguard, a follower of the Fire God. That's why I could not put a spell on them. I bet you I'll beat the next one."

They did not wait long before a magnificent procession came along. It was a procession of Jikei, the archbishop of the Enryaku-ji temple atop Mt. Hiei.

"Oh, here comes a big figure!" Jiro-bo, sur-

prised at the procession of the most learned and
virtuous priest in Japan, felt concerned for the
unsuccessful Chinese goblin, when there suddenly
appeared around Jikei's palanquin from no-one
knew-where a group of five fierce lads.

These lads, wielding a whip each, warned one
another, "Watch out! There lurks a goblin around
here. Don't let him hurt our master!" No sooner
had they uttered the words than they tried to
sight the goblin.

Their action came so fast that Chira Eiju had
no time to get away. All he did was to hover restlessly about. Soon he was caught by them, severely
beaten, and blown off like a leaf in the wind.

"Oh, that hurts! Help me!" he exclaimed. When
Jiro-bo came to him, Chira Eiju grumbled: "That
bonze offered a damn prayer. Those strong
bodyguards! They are the Five Paladins of
Buddha. They have broken my hucklebone. Oh!
Oh!"

So it was that Chira Eiju was beaten by three
noted Japanese magician priests he once had
thought meanly of.

"What a deep disgrace you have brought upon
your own head, after coming all the way from
your country! But you were lucky, because your
long nose, which is our symbol, was not snapped
off," Jiro-bo laughingly said.

It is told that a pair of *tengu* afterward appeared
at a spa somewhere in Japan. We are sure they
must have been Chira Eiju and Jiro-bo, who
probably visited there for treatment.

15. Bewitched
by a boar

IN THE NORTHWESTERN part of Kyoto, there rises a 3,050-foot mountain named Atagoyama. It is the highest mountain among those surrounding the city, and its name is often quoted in local school songs together with another famous mountain, Hieizan, and the Kamo River. From olden times, many faithfuls of the city used to climb up the mountain to pay their monthly visit to Atago Shrine on the top. This shrine is dedicated to the God of Fire Prevention.

An interesting tale is still told about this mountain.

Once upon a time, there lived on the top of Atagoyama an old priest who devoted all his life to the study of Buddhism. Every day he sat upright on a straw mat, with his eyes half-closed, and loudly recited the Lotus Sutra, hour after hour.

Those who knew him believed that he was the holiest priest in the country. To tell the truth, he was just reciting it without understanding its meaning at all. "He might be a learned fool," a Japanese saying goes. At any rate, he was well content with his life on the mountain.

At the foot of this mountain lived a pious old hunter who made his living by shooting deer or boar. As he was well acquainted with the priest, he would call on the latter with some present and have a chat with him.

One day the hunter came up to the priest's abode, bringing some fruit as a gift. The aged bonze, so very pleased with his visit, entertained him warmly, talking of one thing and another for hours. Toward the end of their pleasant conversation, the priest suddenly drew closer to the hunter and said in a low tone, "By the way, my good man, have you ever seen Buddha? These days I have the pleasure of seeing him at night. As you know, I have long devoted myself to the study of Buddhism, so I think my devotion has been rewarded at long last. When it grows dark outside, he appears at this poor cloister. What a majestic scene it is! I sincerely recommend that you stay here tonight and see him, too."

Hearing this story, the hunter exclaimed with astonishment, "What! You say, Buddha makes his holy appearance here. Indeed, I can't believe it. Never! But if what you say is really true, I should like to see him, too."

As recommended by the priest, he decided to stay at the cloister overnight to see the holy figure of Buddha. While waiting for the sunset, he was served supper. When left alone in the room after the meal, he called in a young priest who happened to pass by and asked him whether Buddha had really made his holy appearance there. The young priest replied that what the aged priest had told was true, and that even he himself had seen his holy figure several times. Despite this assurance, he was still doubtful that a common believer like himself could really see Buddha just as the well-trained priest did.

In the meantime, the sun set in the west and it grew dark. In the room the hunter sat up face-to-face with the aged priest and was expecting the mysterious Buddha at any moment. It was not a moonlit night, and not a single star was seen in the sky. All was still and everything was wrapped in darkness. Every now and then, leaves rustled in the wind and tu-whoos were heard among the trees as the night wore on.

Now it was midnight. Suddenly the eastern sky began to brighten up as if the moon were sticking out her round face from behind the clouds. Then this strange brilliance came nearer and nearer toward their place, and several minutes later it came to find its way into the matted room in which the two were sitting. And lo! Up in the splendor there appeared the figure of Holy Buddha riding on the back of a white elephant. It was a very divine spectacle indeed! This resplendent figure, which had come close enough to the building, suddenly stopped its movement in the air.

As for the priest, he, from the beginning of these mysterious happenings, kept himself flat on the floor wrapped in the brilliant presence of Buddha, shedding tears of joy on the mat. The hunter kept watching every movement of the figure with curiosity until the prostrate priest, turning to him, whispered, "Well? Did you see him and bow to him, too?"

"Yes, sir," answered the hunter, hurriedly bending his forehead to the mat.

But he thought, "This is a little funny. It's quite natural that a well-trained priest like him should, with his virtue, be able to see Buddha. But

how could I, who am not practiced in asceticism
at all? Let me see, there must be something fishy
about this Buddha. All right, I'll find it out."

With quick action, he raised himself up, fixed
an arrow to the string of his bow, pulled it as round
as the full moon and shot it out into the darkness.
The arrow flew straight on toward the mysteriously illuminated figure as a piece of iron is attracted
by a magnet, and hit it right in the heart.

All of a sudden the light faded and everything
was covered with darkness. Silence prevailed for
a few seconds. But soon the silence was broken by
a succession of rattling noises. At the unexpected
profane conduct of the hunter, the priest was
so astonished that for a moment he could not
utter a single word.

Regaining his senses after a while, he cried
bitterly, "O you, what a thing you have done!
Could there be greater impiety than this?"

The hunter felt so sorry for him. But as he had
a definite thought in mind, he persuaded the
miserable priest not to cry any more.

"I'm very sorry for you, my respected saint.
When I set my eyes upon his figure, I got an
impression that something was fishy about him.
So I had to find it out by any means. Please don't
cry any more and don't worry about damnation."

Thus he tried all possible ways and means to
console the priest, who was now sunk in deep
sorrow, but in vain. Meanwhile the veil of darkness
began to fade away, and everything was awaking
from its sleep, bit by bit. As soon as it grew light

enough, the hunter stepped down on the ground and approached the spot where the monster had probably been standing on the preceding night.

To his great surprise, the ground there had in a single night turned into a sea of blood. And the marks of blood dotted the soil toward the valley beyond. He carefully traced these bloodstains one hundred yards, walking on the flat ground and climbing down the rocky slope, and found himself at the bottom of the deep valley at last.

There he saw a huge wild boar lying dead, its heart pierced with an arrow. At this horrible sight, the priest who had come after him was astonished, as he saw the true shape of the resplendent Buddha with his own eyes.

Now he did not feel sorrow any longer. He even felt ashamed of himself for believing he had acquired supernatural power through many years of learning.

It is told that there have not been any more mysterious events of that kind on the mountain since then.

16. A cat-hater

LONG, LONG AGO, there was in the capital a peculiar person named Fujiwara Kiyokado. He was an official of the department of finance and held the court rank of *goi* (fifth grade).

He was a great hater of cats and was so much afraid of these animals that he was nicknamed "Human Rat." Half for fun, some of his friends would scare him by putting cats beside him. Even in the office he would run away abandoning his work at the sight of a cat. The officials of the department therefore called him "Cat-hating Kiyokado."

Kiyokado was a rich man with large estates in Yamato, Yamashiro, and Iga provinces. But he would not pay taxes to the government of Yamato Province. In olden times people offered bags of rice as taxes to the provincial governments. The officials of the Yamato government requested many times that Kiyokado pay the taxes, but he would not pay them.

One day Governor Sukegimi and his men got together to study the best way to make the cat-hater pay taxes.

"If we leave this matter unsettled, he will never pay the taxes. We must do something."

"As he is a *goi*-holder, we cannot punish him merely for not paying. He will be crafty enough to make some excuse for his neglect of payment."

They were at a loss what to do with Kiyokado. All of a sudden the governor hit upon a good idea. Just then Kiyokado accidentally came to see the governor, who immediately had him shown into his office and the door locked. Then the 'governor began politely, "Dear Kiyokado, why don't you pay the taxes? I have been strictly instructed by the central government to collect them from you. I ask you to tell your estate managers to pay the taxes without delay."

"I am very sorry to trouble you, dear Sukegimi. I have been so busy that I was compelled to put off the payment. Since it is our duty to pay the taxes, I promise I will pay them in the near future."

Although cat-hating Kiyokado apparently apologized to the governor, he cried in his heart that he would never tender a single grain of rice to the government. Governor Sukegimi, however, was not deceived at all, for he was well aware of the cat-hater's tactics.

"My friend Kiyokado, you cannot fool me this time. You promised me many times that you would pay the taxes, but you never kept your word. I do wish to settle this problem today. If you will not accept my request, I will not let you out," said Sukegimi.

"Please don't get excited, Governor Sukegimi. Though I have said I would pay them in the near future, I promise you I will pay them by the end of this month. Is that satisfactory to you?"

"No, no, I cannot trust you." The governor continued, "As we have been close friends for many years, I do not wish to have trouble with you. I will let bygones be bygones. Again I ask you to pay the taxes at once."

Kiyokado, however, held out persistently. "As I told you, I am in no position to pay them right now. I have to talk with my managers about how to pay."

The governor became excited by his indecisive attitude and cried, "Guards, bring them in!" Kiyokado, remaining calm, wondered what the governor's men would bring into the room. In a minute, there was heard a meowing in the doorway, and a big grey cat came in. She was followed by four others.

"Oh, cats! No, no. Take them out, please," cried Kiyokado, with a tremble. He earnestly asked the governor, with joined hands, to take out the animals right away.

The cats came near the stranger, meowing, and one of them got on his lap while another jumped on his shoulder. A third took a sniff of the sleeves of his kimono, and others ran about the room.

Kiyokado was quite helpless. He looked pale, trembling with fear. At this sight, the governor thought that his tactics had worked well.

"Guards, take them out," he ordered. The cats were immediately taken out and tied with strings to the door post. Unable to move freely, they began a meowing chorus which immensely tortured the cat-hater. He was in a cold sweat and felt more dead than alive.

"Well, dear Kiyokado. Do you still wish to put off the payment?"

"Oh, help me, Governor! I will do anything you want me to do. Please take them away!"

"All right. I will have them taken away. But before doing that, I must request you to write a letter to your estate managers. Tell them to pay the taxes today. If you fail to meet my request, I must tell my guards to bring in the cats again."

"Oh, no! I'll surely die of shock to death if I see them again. I will be very happy to write a letter."

Whereupon the governor had brush and ink brought in for Kiyokado's use. The cat-hater, thus pressed, had no other choice but to write a letter telling his managers to tender immediately five hundred rice bags to the provincial government of Yamato.

This interesting story soon spread in the capital and people congratulated the witty governor on his splendid victory over the cat-hater.

17. The flying water jars

WITH THE COMING of autumn, many hundreds of thousands of Kyotoites turn out on each holiday and visit noted maple-viewing resorts in the suburbs of the city.

One of these resorts is Takao, which lies several miles up the clear stream of Kiyotaki River. The deep valley is entirely covered with red leaves of maple trees in this season, and presents a fantastic view. On both sides of the stream are many improvised resting booths in a row, and visitors may open their lunch boxes, or have a maple-viewing party, merrily laughing and talking, or singing with the accompaniment of strolling musicians.

At some distance from the stream stands a Buddhist temple called Jingo-ji, which was founded in 824 by Kobo Daishi, one of the most revered Buddhist priests and the founder of the Shingon sect of Buddhism.

Now here is an interesting tale about this stream.

Long, long ago, there lived near this stream a priest who had been studying Buddhism for a long time. Through his continued self-imposed penance, he acquired such wonderful magic power that he could make a jar fetch water from the river. He was proud of being so great a priest.

One day, he saw another jar come flying from the upper reaches of the river, fill itself with water, and fly back. Several days later, he again saw the jar do the same work and fly back. He could hardly believe that anyone capable of such magic lived up the river. So he promptly ran for several miles up along the river after the jar, and saw it finally go into the hut of a small cloister. Its roof and the garden were covered with moss, and presented a kind of holiness. When he noiselessly stepped up to a window and looked into the room, he saw a sacred book left open on the desk and even smelled incense burning.

He carefully took another look around the room, and found an old noble-looking priest dozing over an elbow rest. To test his magic power, the younger priest drew close to him with stealthy steps and chanted a spell of fire evil. The old priest, even in his sleep, took up a cane, soaked it in holy water, which he sprinkled all around himself. Some drops fell on the younger priest and set his robe on fire.

Frightened, he ran out to the garden and tried to beat out the fire. The holy priest, awakened from his sleep by the noise, saw the younger one in trouble, so he sprinkled more water on him. This mysterious shower put the fire out in a moment, so he was saved from being burned to death.

Stepping up to him, the holy priest asked, "Why have you come here to meet such trouble?" The younger priest answered:

"I am a priest living several miles down the river. I was confident that I was the only priest capable of using magic, until I saw another jar drawing water from the river and realized that there was someone else who could do the same. To find out who he was, I came here following the jar, and found you dozing in the room. I tried to do some mischief to you, but instead I found myself in trouble. You are far greater than I, and you have opened my eyes. I humbly apologize to you for my ill conduct. Please let me be your follower."

At this, the aged priest granted his request and made him his follower. This tale teaches us the lesson that we must not be conceited.

18. Grave
of the chopstick

LONG, LONG AGO, there was a very beautiful princess in this country. Since she was the only daughter of the emperor and empress, she was raised with the deepest affection and utmost care which are usual with the Japanese.

One night, when she was in her bedroom, a handsome lad stole in and proposed to her. "How could a decent girl simply accept the proposal of a stranger without the consent of her parents?" The princess rebuffed him politely.

But the lad came night after night and earnestly proposed to her, saying, "Even though your father and mother came to know our secret connection, I am sure they would never oppose it." Despite his persistent proposal, the princess would not give him her consent.

As time went by, however, the princess gradually found it difficult to resist. She therefore talked over the matter with her father and mother, who then thought that the lad could not be an ordinary person to steal into the heavily guarded palace every night and propose to her. They imagined that this mysterious intruder must be a deity incarnate. A deity incarnate! At that, the princess felt obliged to give herself to the stranger. From that night, the two became inseparable. But, strange to say, the princess still knew nothing about the man, even his name and rank.

One night, when he came, she said, "My dear, I am sorry I have not yet been told anything about you. I think we should open our hearts. Don't you think so?"

The young man replied, "I am one who is always near you. If you are so eager to know something about me, I suggest you to look into your small oil bottle tomorrow morning. Then, you will find out who I am. But I give you a warning: Don't be startled at what is in the bottle. If you do, I should be obliged to part from you forever. Please remember that."

The girl wondered about the strange remark, but made a promise that she wouldn't be startled by anything in the bottle. When day broke, the man faded away.

Time came when the princess was to open the bottle. When she took off the lid and looked in, she found a very small white snake coiling its body at the bottom! At that, the princess became frightened. With a shriek, she dropped the bottle on the floor and ran out of the room. That her lover should be a small snake!

That night, the lad came as usual. But he was in ill humor. He would not even come near the princess. She wondered what was the matter with him. Coldly he said, "My dear girl, you have broken your promise. I am disappointed in you. As I told you before, I am obliged to part from you."

With that, he was ready to go. The princess was surprised and, clinging to his sleeve, implored, "I am very sorry. Please forgive me. I swear that I never will do that again. So, please do not go away."

For a moment, the princess struggled with the

lad to keep him from going, but in vain. The lad, forcibly thrusting her away, vanished. How sad she was! The princess now lost what she lived for. In despair, she took a sharp chopstick, struck it into her heart, and died.

The emperor and empress grieved deeply over her death and buried her body somewhere on the outskirts of Nara. It is told that at the site where her body was buried, there was erected a tombstone which people later called "Hashi no Haka" (Grave of the Chopstick).

19. The bell thieves

LONG, LONG AGO, in the province of Settsu (now Hyogo Prefecture), there was an old Buddhist temple called Koya-dera.

One day an old priest about eighty years of age visited this temple. He had a cane in one hand and a big straw hat in the other. It was near sunset.

"*Otanomi mosu* (Hello there)," he cried at the doorway. But no response came from within the house. The priest therefore went round to the side door and called out again. Then a voice called, "Who is it?" and a priest came out. He seemed to be the chief priest of the temple.

"I am from a western province and on my way to the capital. A long journey has made me so tired that I cannot walk farther today. As I am too old to sleep under the open sky, please give me shelter for the night," the itinerant priest implored.

"I am very sorry for you, but we have no vacant rooms tonight. How about seeking a lodging at other places?" the temple priest suggested. Then, the old priest asked permission to stay in the belfry and offered bell-ringing service in return. The chief priest was pleased to accept his offer and conducted him to the bell tower.

For two days from that night, the bell was rung by the aged priest. On the third day, however, for unknown reasons there was no toll of the bell. So one of the temple priests visited the tower to see what was the matter with the lodger. As he opened the door, he was surprised to see the old priest lying on the floor. He was dead.

"The lodger is dead!" he cried.

The abbot, much surprised, immediately came with his followers to the belfry. They consulted about how to dispose of his body. After a long discussion they decided to ask the villagers to bury the body in the village cemetery. But the villagers declined their request because they said they could not profane their tutelary deity by touching the dead body before celebrating the coming feast. Their refusal greatly embarrassed the priests.

The next day there was a loud voice "Tanomo!" at the entrance of the temple. The chief priest came out and found a couple of young samurai in traveling outfits standing at the doorway. They asked if he had seen an old priest who had traveled near the temple. The chief priest therefore gave them a full account of the dead priest and said that the whole temple was at a loss how to dispose of his body.

"Dead!"

The young samurai were greatly surprised at the account and collapsed on the spot. So the chief priest asked who they were.

"The dead priest is our father. He was disposed to ramble and frequently disappeared from our home. Recently he left home again and so we were looking for him. As he is now dead, we wish to hold a funeral for him."

When the young men saw their father's body, they wept bitterly over it. They said they would come again at night to carry the body to the cemetery. So the chief priest was very pleased to have them claim the body.

About eight o'clock in the evening, the stillness of the temple compound was suddenly broken by a noisy crowd of men who came to carry the body from the belfry. As the priests had nothing to do with the body, they remained in the house and listened to the noises outdoors. Before long, the crowd seemed to have carried the body into the pine forest behind the temple, for the priests heard their prayers accompanied by drum and bell coming from there. They conducted the noisy ceremony all the night through.

As day broke, the noises were no longer heard and the crowd seemed to have gone away. In those days it was the custom for people to stay away for a month from the house where a person had died, so the temple priests would not visit the belfry during the mourning period.

After a month had passed, one of the priests came to the tower. He opened the door and was astonished to see . . .

"Oh, the bell's gone!"

He found nothing but a straw mat left on the floor. Since the tower had been closed for a long time, the air was damp and the room was full of cobwebs. He ran back to report the incident to the abbot.

"Nonsense! Who could carry away the bell? It is too heavy to be moved," cried the chief priest. Thereupon all the priests came to the belfry and found the bell gone. They were amazed at the extraordinary strength of the thief.

"Who could carry it away?"

"Say, I suspect the mourners. They must have taken it."

"I see. But, what were they doing in the forest? Let us go to see the place."

The priests immediately went to the forest. Many trees had been cut down and apparently burned to melt down the bell, for the priests found pieces of melted metal scattered on the ground. They all admired the thieves' trick.

"The old priest pretended to be dead all day. I don't think any other thief could do it so well."

"No one else could pretend to weep so bitterly as the young men. They made us shed tears of sympathy."

"They were very clever indeed, in making noises overnight to divert our attention from their destruction of the bell."

"Anyway, they were good strategists."

The Koya-dera thus lost its treasure bell for good and all.

20. The monkey's gratitude

LONG, LONG AGO, in a fishing hamlet in Kyushu, there lived an honest fisherman with his wife and their baby.

One day, when the tide was out, his wife with the baby on her back went out with her neighbors to gather shells. As the weather was very fine, many persons were gathering shells on the beach.

The fisherman's wife put her baby on a huge rock, asked a neighbor's boy to look after it, and set to work. As she was gathering shells, she found a monkey playing on the beach. The animal apparently had come from a nearby mountain.

"Look! There is a monkey over there. I wonder what he is doing. Let us go and see," she said. They went together to see the monkey, but, strangely, the animal would not run away. At their approaching steps, the monkey looked about restlessly but still remained there. It appeared that he was unable to set himself free from something.

"What is the matter with him? It is very strange that he does not run away."

As they came to the monkey, they found his hand caught in a big closed shell.

"Ha, ha! It seems that as he tried to pull the flesh out of the open shell, it closed on his hand."

The monkey was desperately struggling to pull out his hand, while the shell tried to bury itself deeper into the sand. It was a very interesting sight indeed. One of the neighbors suddenly picked up a big stone and tried to kill him with it. She hated the monkey because he frequently damaged the farms. The fisherman's wife, however, took pity on the animal and asked the neighbor to spare his life.

Meanwhile, the tide began to rise and violent waves came dashing ashore. The monkey had great trouble battling with the shell, rolling about on the beach and splashing the water about him. The other shell-gatherers had already stopped their work and gone home.

The kind-hearted wife forced open the shell and freed the monkey's hand. She also pitied the shell. Instead of picking it up, she softly buried it in the wet sand.

"I warn you, monkey, not to destroy the farms any more," said the wife. The monkey appeared to have understood what she had said. The next instant, however, he suddenly jumped onto the huge rock and, picking up her baby, ran away with it toward the mountain.

The woman was astonished at the animal's act and angrily cried that the animal had returned evil for good. She did not lose a second in chasing it in order to take back her baby. Her neighbors also ran after the monkey, saying that it did her no good to spare his life.

The monkey, with the baby in his arms, ran so fast that the mother could not catch up with him. She called out for the immediate return of her baby. But the monkey still kept running and finally climbed a tall tree. The mother and her neighbors soon arrived at the foot of the tree. The monkey was sitting on a branch, so the people could do nothing but look up at him. One of the neighbors went back to tell the incident to the baby's father.

In the meantime, the monkey, with the baby in his right arm, began to sway the branch with his left hand. The baby was surprised at his violent act and began crying. At this dangerous sight, the mother felt as if her heart were breaking.

Just then, a big eagle came swooping down from the top of the mountain beyond. The people feared that the bird would snatch the baby from the monkey and eat it. The baby's mother closed her eyes and earnestly prayed to Buddha for his help.

As the eagle swooped down upon the monkey, the monkey suddenly released his left hand which had pulled the branch hard, as if to draw a bow to the full. The branch sprang back with strong force, striking the head of the eagle. The big bird was instantly killed and dropped headfirst to the ground. Then the monkey pulled the branch again. As another eagle came swooping down the wise monkey again counterattacked it, knocking it down instantly. The people anxiously watched this peculiar battle. In a short while, five eagles were successively struck down to the ground.

It seems that as the monkey struggled with the shell on the beach, he had noticed the eagles watching for an opportunity to snatch away the baby on the rock. So, after he was released from the shell, he protected the baby from the eagles' attacks in return for the woman's kindness.

The danger gone, the monkey quickly came

down from the tree and gently placed the baby on the ground, then went up again. The people could now understand the monkey's motivation. The baby's father soon came and was given a complete account of what had happened. After this the villagers happily went home together.

It is said that the fisherman later obtained much money by selling the beautiful wings of the dead eagles to a rich man in town.

21. The lost dinner

IN THE NORTHWESTERN part of Kyoto, there rise in a line three hills named Narabi-ga-Oka, or Triple Hills. Their tops are covered with pine trees. At some distance from the foot of the hills stands Ninna-ji Temple, one of the famous temples of the Shingon sect of Buddhism.

About these hills an interesting tale is still told. Many a hundred years ago a page was serving at the temple. He was so cute that some priests planned one day to take him out to the hills on a picnic and play a trick on him.

Before starting for the picnic, they fixed some dinner, which they put in a picnic box and secretly buried at a certain spot on one of the hills.

"Say, dear boy. You are serving us very well every day. Now and then you need some recreation. It's a very fine day so we are planning to go to Narabi-ga-Oka for some fun. How about coming with us?" they said to the little one.

The boy accepted their offer at once. They all went out together after obtaining permission from the chief priest.

They walked around on the hills, enjoying the nice view and the fresh air of the fine autumn weather, and came to the spot where the priests had previously buried the picnic dinner box.

"Oh, I'm tired. Let's rest here," said one of them, and the others, as planned, agreed to his idea. Another one said, "I'm hungry. If any one of you have the magic power to dig up a dinner by simply chanting a prayer, I'd appreciate it."

"All right. I'll try. You just watch," said the third one instantly, and began to recite something loudly, rubbing the beads of his rosary, as if to chant a prayer to Buddha.

Several minutes later, he finished his sham prayer and said with an air of importance, "During my prayer, I received a divine revelation. I was told to dig here to find a dinner for us."

At this, the other priests started digging up the spot to take out their previously buried dinner box. The innocent page watched what they did with curiosity and doubt.

Contrary to their expectation, however, they did not find the box there. They wondered if they might have dug in the wrong spot, so they, with many pains, dug here and there all over the place. But they could not find anything that resembled the box at all.

Quite exhausted with hard labor, they sat down on the ground, struck dumb with the unexpected turn of events. With the coming of darkness, they made their way back to the temple, quite downcast by the failure of their trick and the loss of their dinner. It is said that someone who had seen them put the dinner box into the ground mischievously took it away during their absence.

22. Reunion
with death

Long, long ago, there lived in the capital a masterless samurai and his wife. In those days things were so bad that he could not easily get a livelihood—that is, he could not find a master to serve. Therefore, the couple lived in dire poverty.

One day he was told that his closest friend had fortunately been appointed as a local administrator and was busy making preparations for departure to his new post. So he set out at once to the friend's residence to tender greetings on his promotion. The friend, though quite busy giving instructions to his retainers for the departure, was glad to see this samurai and had a little talk with him.

Toward the end of their friendly conversations, the friend said, "By the way, my dearest friend, what are you going to do from now on? I know you have long been seeking a position here in the capital. But as you know, times are hard now. So I am afraid nobody will give you a position easily. As your closest friend, I sincerely recommend that you come with me. I am sure I can help you somehow at my new post. I have been hoping to help you but until now I was not in a position to do so. Now I have fortunately been promoted to the post of local administrator. So I think I can help you. You can't go on like this—without getting any position. So, think it over."

"Thank you very much for your kind offer, my dear friend. To tell you the truth, we are badly off now, though my wife does not complain about our hard living. I should be much obliged if you would give me any position under your command." Expressing his deepest gratitude to the friend, this samurai accepted the kind offer on the spot.

Poor as he was, he had been enjoying a happy life with his beloved wife, who was young and beautiful and had a tender heart. They did not let poverty pull out the wedge of love between them. Therefore he found it very hard to depart for the local post alone because of financial difficulty.

Just before his departure, however, in secret he immorally married another woman, who had vast property and had offered to help him financially. He left the capital with her—leaving his devoted wife behind, alone.

In the remote province, he was set free from the feelings of poverty for many years and indulged in luxury with the second wife, forgetting to send even a single letter to the wife left behind in the capital. In this way, many a year passed.

However, he sometimes in a quiet hour thought about his present mode of life and felt guilty for enjoying a luxurious life with another woman while his poor wife was left alone at home without getting any allowance from him. As time went by, his heart ached more and more with longing for her. So anxious was he to see her again that he could not settle to his work even for a single moment, just hoping for the early arrival of the day to return to the capital. And that day came at long last!

On his way back home, feeling deep guilt for having lived a double life with another woman, he made up his mind to humbly apologize to his wife by confessing everything, and though poor, to enjoy life with her again. Upon his arrival in the capital, he parted from the second wife and went straight back to his old home.

The house was precisely at the place where it had stood before. The gate was wide open. One weather-beaten door hung from a rusty hinge; the other had been carried away somewhere. The roof was covered with weeds and moss, and ridge tiles had fallen to pieces on the ground.

With a glimpse of the desolate building, a sense of gloom pervaded his spirit. Once through the gate, he found the garden utterly neglected and all the doors of the house closed. There was no sign of human habitation.

It was the night of the twentieth day of the ninth month. The moon was casting her soft, silvery light upon everything, weeds were swaying in the autumn breeze, and crickets were chirping here and there.

Pushing off one of the sliding doors, he stepped into the dark house and examined the rooms one after another, and lo! there in the living room sat his beloved wife looking toward him. "Welcome home, my dear husband! I have been expecting your return every day. I missed you very much," she said faintly, showing a sweet smile on her beautiful face.

Received in such an unexpectedly warm

manner, he felt relieved and told her how anxious
he had been to see her, saying, "Now that we are
together again in this house I never wish to part
from you. I don't want anything except you. You
are everything to me."

As night was far advanced, they went to bed
together. "By the way, my darling, did you live
here all by yourself during my absence?" asked
the samurai.

"Yes, I lived alone, as you say. I did not have
any source of income, so I had to cut down the
cost of living as much as possible. To employ a
servant was far beyond my means."

Poor thing! How sadly she had lived in such a
lonely house! The more he felt pity for her, the
wider he was kept awake. It was around dawn
when he finally fell asleep. When he awoke, it
was broad daylight and the sun was streaming into
the dark room through the chinks in the doors.

"Now, let us get up, darling," said the samurai,
and turned toward the wife. Behold! There beside
him lay—a dead body, now a mere bag of bones!
Springing to his feet with a shriek, he rushed
out into the garden, breaking down a sliding
door. When once again he looked into the room,
there still lay the dead body! He stood in dismay
for a moment. But soon he came to his senses
and went to a neighbor's house and asked, "Excuse
me, but may I ask something about the house over
there? Would you tell me who lives in that house?"

The neighbor gazed at his face for a moment
and then said, "That house! Don't you know any-

thing about that house? All right, I will tell you a story. Many many years ago, a poor samurai and his beautiful wife lived a happy life in that house. One day the samurai left to take a position in a local administrative office, leaving his beloved wife behind. Many months and years passed and yet not a single letter came from him. However, the faithful wife led a life of misery, vainly waiting day after day for a call from her husband.

"Some time ago, a rumor spread in the neighborhood that the samurai was indulging in luxury, living with another woman far away at his post, and not giving a thought to his poor wife at home. Oh, what a wretch! Hearing this, the wife grieved so deeply over her ill fate that she passed away this summer after a long illness. Poor woman! As she had neither relatives nor friends to hold a funeral service for her, her dead body has been lying untouched in that gloomy house."

People of those days told one another that the dead wife must have returned from beyond the grave to attain a long-cherished desire to see her dear husband again.

—THE END—